SKYLARK CHOOSE YOUR OWN ADVENTURE® • 51

"I DON'T LIKE CHOOSE YOUR OWN AD-VENTURE® BOOKS. I *LOVE* THEM!" says Jessica Gordon, age ten. And now, kids between the ages of six and nine can choose their own adventures too. Here's what kids have to say about the Skylark Choose Your Own Adventure® books.

"These are my favorite books because you can pick whatever choice you want—and the story is all about you."
—**Katy Alson,** *age 8*

"I love finding out how my story will end."
—**Josh Williams,** *age 9*

"I like all the illustrations!"
—**Savitri Brightfield,** *age 7*

"A six-year-old friend and I have lots of fun making the decisions together."
—**Peggy Marcus** *(adult)*

Bantam Skylark Books in the Choose Your Own Adventure® Series
Ask your bookseller for the books you have missed

YOU CAN MAKE A DIFFERENCE:
THE STORY OF
MARTIN LUTHER KING, JR.

ANNE BAILEY

ILLUSTRATED BY LESLIE MORRILL

An Edward Packard Book

A BANTAM SKYLARK BOOK"
NEW YORK · TORONTO · LONDON · SYDNEY · AUCKLAND

RL 2, 007–009

YOU CAN MAKE A DIFFERENCE:
THE STORY OF MARTIN LUTHER KING, JR.
A Bantam Skylark Book / February 1990

*Cover art by Bill Schmidt
Interior illustrations by Leslie Morrill*

*Bantam Books are published by Bantam Books, a division of Bantam
Doubleday Dell Publishing Group, Inc. Its trademark, consisting of the
words "Bantam Books" and the portrayal of a rooster, is Registered in
U.S. Patent and Trademark Office and in other countries. Marca Reg-
istrada. Bantam Books, 666 Fifth Avenue, New York, New York
10103.*

PRINTED IN THE UNITED STATES OF AMERICA

O   0 9 8 7 6 5 4 3 2 1

For my mother, Daphne Bailey,
because you have made all the
difference in my life.

The author wishes to thank
Harry Wachtel, Clayton Riley,
Charles Kochman, and Edward
Packard for their help and
assistance.

READ THIS FIRST!!!

Most books are about other people.

This book is about you, and what happens to you as you celebrate Martin Luther King, Jr.'s, birthday.

Do not read this book from the first page through to the last. Instead, start on page one and read until you come to your first choice. Then decide what you want to do, turn to the page shown, and see what happens.

When you come to the end of a story, go back and start another. Every choice leads to a new adventure.

Are you ready to join Martin Luther King, Jr., in his fight for civil rights? Then turn to page one—and good luck!

Imagine that you live in a warm cozy home **1** in Atlanta, Georgia. You and your family have lived here for as long as you can remember. Behind the house is a large backyard. On lazy days you like to swing in the hammock that hangs over your mother's rose garden.

Today is Martin Luther King, Jr.'s, birthday. Tonight you will be celebrating with your family. You love birthday parties, and you are looking forward to this one. But you wonder why you are celebrating the birthday of someone you don't know.

Turn to page 2.

2   After you have finished your dinner, you ask your mother where the cake is. "No birthday party is any good without a cake," you say.

Your mother smiles as she goes off to the kitchen and brings back two things: a book, and a big cake with many colorful candles burning on it.

"Who is Martin, Mommy?" your little sister asks. "Is he coming to the party?" Everybody laughs.

Turn to page 8.

4   Suddenly you wake up, and you are lying in your bed, rubbing your eyes. What a dream! You'll never forget it.

Later that day, as you watch your sister running up to a nearby water fountain, you think about your dream the night before.

"You see," your mother says to you and your sister, "Martin Luther King, Jr., is with us even now. There are no signs at this water fountain telling you that you can't drink here. And every time you get on the bus, you can sit anywhere you like. And wherever you go to eat, no matter how plain or how fancy, you can expect to be given a seat and served the same as anyone else."

Your mother's words are comforting. By looking all around you at the things you take for granted, you realize what a difference Martin Luther King, Jr., made on your life!

The End

You decide to play at the fire station. You **7** say good-bye to your father and run there as fast as you can. You spot the big fire truck parked out front. No one is looking, so you hide behind the truck, and then climb right into the driver's seat. You are going to put out a big fire on Auburn Avenue, you pretend.

"Out of my way!" you yell, sounding the siren. It's louder than you imagined.

"Now what are you doing here again?" asks your favorite fire fighter with a smile. "You know that we've got work to do."

He pulls you out of the truck, and sends you on your way home. That was fun, you think. Now what?

You love to play. In fact, you love to play with your sister.

One day you are teasing her a little too long and a little too hard. Your brother tries to stop you. You get angry, as you sometimes do when you don't get your way, and you hit him over the head with a telephone. As he falls to the ground, you look on in shock. Frightened by what you have done, you run away.

Turn to page 19.

8   Your mother motions for you and your sister to sit on the sofa in the living room. Then she opens the book.

"Martin Luther King, Jr., is no longer alive, but I'm going to tell you why we celebrate his birthday every year at this time."

Both you and your sister listen carefully.

"He was born on January 15, 1929, on Auburn Avenue right here in Atlanta," your mother begins. She then tells you the story of Martin Luther King, Jr.—of who he was and all that he did.

"Our world would be a very different place if he had never been born," your mother says at the end of the story. "By believing strongly in himself, and standing by what he believed in, he was able to change the world."

Turn to page 16.

You decide to continue being the leader of the boycott despite the threats. It was a hard decision, but you feel you can't let the people of Montgomery down.

The boycott lasts over a year. Finally, in November 1956, the Supreme Court of the United States rules that segregation on city buses is against the law. This is a great victory. All along you have believed that if you remained true to yourself and what you believed in, good would win out.

The first day, when blacks can sit wherever they want to on the city buses, is a happy one. The civil rights movement has begun.

Turn to page 38.

10   You go to a downtown shoe store with your father. As you walk into the store, a salesperson says, "Whites in the front, blacks in the back."

Your father, a proud man, takes your hand and walks out.

"Why couldn't we buy my shoes there, Daddy?" you ask on the way home.

"I will not give my money to a store that treats people differently because of the color of their skin," he says. "That's called *racism,* and I have fought it all my life. Will you join me?"

"Yes, Daddy, I will," you say. "I will help you all I can."

Turn to page 40.

12   It is not until months later, in August 1965, that a law is passed guaranteeing all blacks the right to vote.

On your fifty-mile march from Selma back to Montgomery, Alabama, you look out on the road ahead of you. You are reminded of the promise you made to your father when you were younger. You said you would help fight racism and prejudice. You could not imagine then all that you would have to do, but now your path is clear.

By the time you reach Montgomery, there are 25,000 marchers behind you, singing, "Oh, deep in my heart I do believe, we shall overcome someday . . . ."

Turn to page 34.

You set up a meeting with the city leaders for the following week. You meet with the mayor and some businessmen.

"Can't you see that the time has come to change the laws that separate blacks and whites?" you say. "Don't you understand—"

"No, it's *you* who does not understand," one city leader says. "If you Negroes would only wait . . ."

"We are tired of waiting," you say. "We have waited long enough."

The mayor bangs loudly on the table. "The buses will remain segregated. Blacks in the back and whites in the front. And if you know what's good for you, you'll tell your people not to boycott!"

You now see that you are left with no choice. The blacks of Montgomery must boycott the buses until the law is changed.

Turn to page 24.

16   That night as you settle in for bed, you think about the differences he made. You try to imagine what it would have been like to be Martin Luther King, Jr.

Soon you fall asleep and begin to drift softly into a dream.

If you dream that you are Martin Luther King, Jr., when he was growing up, turn to page 43.

If you dream about what the world would have been like had he never lived, turn to page 28.

18   Your parents sit you down and tell you about *segregation*—how people are separated because of the color of their skin. They also tell you about *slavery*—how your ancestors were brought over to America from Africa and were forced to work for others. "But you are as good as anyone," your mother tells you. "Always be proud of who you are."

These words are comforting, but you are still upset. To cheer you up, your father tells you that he will either take you downtown to buy something, or, if you like, to the drugstore for an ice-cream soda.

If you decide to go downtown and shop,
turn to page 10.

If you decide to have an ice-cream soda,
turn to page 21.

Your father finds you hiding behind a tree in your friend Billy's backyard. You go home with him, feeling bad about hitting your brother. Billy trails behind.

In your bedroom, you wait for your mother to come home. You know you're going to be punished.

"What does *that* mean?" Billy asks, pointing to the three large *S*'s on your bedroom wall.

Turn to page 37.

You decide to go to the drugstore for an ice-cream soda. That will cheer you up.

"I want a chocolate one," you say to the black woman behind the counter. "The biggest ice-cream soda you have."

"It's been a hard day for you," your father says, softly. "Maybe when you are a minister like me, you'll be able to help bring about some changes in the way people are treated."

"I don't know if I want to be a minister, Dad," you say, taking a big slurp out of your soda. Right now you are not ready for such ideas.

Finishing the last of your soda, you ask your father if you can go. You really feel like playing at the fire station. You love playing in the engine. You dream of one day becoming a fire fighter. Then you remember that you promised your mother you would help her around the house when you got back.

*If you play at the fire station,
turn to page 7.*

*If you go home to help your mother,
turn to page 27.*

As a minister, you are first assigned to Dexter Avenue Baptist Church in Montgomery, Alabama. Now is your chance to apply all that you have studied.

You are not in Montgomery long when a woman named Rosa Parks, a seamstress, is arrested on December 1, 1955. She had worked long and hard and did not want to give up her seat on the bus and stand. She was very tired. She knew that the law of segregation in the South that separated blacks and whites was wrong. So she remained seated rather than give up her seat to a white passenger.

Turn to page 41.

24   You agree to boycott the buses and lead the blacks of Montgomery, Alabama. The people set up car pools. They take taxis and ride bicycles. Many people walk to and from work. Many of the white people in the city, however, do not like this idea at all. They do what they can to stop the boycott. Buses all across the city that are usually filled with thousands of black riders are now almost empty.

In the meantime you speak to the people, uniting their spirit. You are amazed at how they listen to you. When you call for a nonviolent protest, they agree with you. The movement is peaceful, and every day the people grow more and more united.

As the boycott continues, you begin to receive threats on your life and the lives of your family. You wonder whether you should continue this boycott or step down as leader.

If you continue the boycott despite the threats, turn to page 9.

If you step down as leader, turn to page 50.

26   You are heartbroken. You really wanted to go on the rides. You can hear kids laughing and having fun. It doesn't seem fair to you that you can't join them.

"I don't understand, Dad. Why are those signs everywhere? I've seen them on the downtown water fountains, too. And the other day when no one was looking, I tried water from both the *white* fountain and the *colored* fountain. They tasted the same."

Your father looks at you sadly. "They are the same," he says. "And black people and white people *are* equal. It's just that there are some people who think they are better than others. Maybe one day things will be different. Then you will be free to do what you want."

Turn to page 33.

You decide to go home and help your mother around the house. You promised her you would help get the living room ready for one of the many community meetings that are held at your house.

You are finished sooner than you expected, so you lie down on the couch.

Now you dream about growing up. In high school you enter public-speaking contests. On one trip out of town you win a prize. This makes you very happy. However, on your way home, you are forced to ride in the back of the bus. This makes you want to fight racism all the more.

Turn to page 31.

28   The moon casts a pale band of light across your blanket, and you begin to dream about what the world would have been like had Martin Luther King, Jr., never lived.

It's Saturday, and you are watching television. A man wearing a tall black hat and a tuxedo says, *"Playland Amusement Park. The place to be for all kids. Roller coasters. Fun houses. A haunted house. And much, much more! Come one, come all!"*

You get excited and want to go. You rush into the bedroom and ask your father if he will take you there tomorrow. He says he was planning to visit your aunt and uncle, but it's up to you.

You love playing with your cousins. But you'd also like to go to the amusement park.

If you decide to go to the amusement park, turn to page 44.

If you decide to visit your cousins, turn to page 46.

Later you attend Morehouse College, where your father went to school. It is there that you are inspired to become a minister, reading books about famous men like Mahatma Gandhi, the Indian leader. He believed in love instead of violence and, by protesting non-violently, he helped win freedom for his people. You see a connection between two important set of values that are to guide you in your life—your religious faith and your belief in nonviolence. By following Gandhi's example, you feel you can also help people.

Turn to page 23.

32 By 1964 you are famous all over the world for the work that you have done to win equal rights for blacks in America.

To your surprise you are awarded one of the highest honors in the world—the Nobel Peace Prize. For you, the award is a reminder that there is still more work to be done for freedom.

You begin work to obtain the right to vote for blacks in the South. In protest, you and your friends march peacefully through the city of Selma, Alabama. There you are met by violence and hatred.

Turn to page 12.

A moment later you wake up with a start, **33** almost crying as you think about what happened to you in your dream. Then you remember that Martin Luther King, Jr., *was* born, and you realize what a difference his life did make.

The End

34   Eventually all your efforts in the nineteen sixties are directed toward a Poor People's Campaign, where you attend to the needs of the poor, in particular their need for jobs. Blacks from the ghettos of the northern cities, Indians from the Southwest, and poor whites from Appalachia will be marching side by side to join you at the steps of the Lincoln Memorial in Washington, D.C. Once again you express your feeling that black or white, rich or poor, we are all the same. That's why we have to help one another.

While you are in your motel room in Memphis, planning the march, you step out on the balcony to get some fresh air. The next thing you know, you've been shot! Suddenly all the threats on your life have come true!

Turn to page 4.

"That's one of our family rules," you say. **37**
"All the money that we make has to be divided up according to the three *S*'s. The first *S* is for *sharing*—I have to share my paper-route money with my brother and sister. The second *S* is for *saving,* and the third *S* is for *spending.*"

"Wow! You have to share your money with your brother and sister? That's terrible."

"It's not terrible," your mother says as she comes in the room. "By following this rule, Billy, we learn to understand the meaning of sharing within the family and with others."

Your mother has always been fair and kind. As she sends Billy home, you can only hope that she will be fair and kind with you and your punishment.

The End

38   In Birmingham, Alabama, at this time, blacks are still segregated. They are not allowed to sit at the same lunch counters that whites are. They can't even drink from the same water fountains. Stores do not have to hire blacks, and sometimes refuse to serve them. These are called Jim Crow laws, and you decide to march against them.

On one of your first marches you are met by the police commissioner Bull Connor and his officers. They put you under arrest and take you to jail. You refuse to give up. You call on the people to march through the streets of Birmingham in protest. Soon your efforts for equality begin to work. At last store owners take down the Whites Only signs from their windows and drinking fountains, and open their stores to everyone!

Turn to page 49.

40   Your ride home is mostly silent. You don't know what will happen, but you feel safe, just as you feel at Ebenezer Baptist Church where you listen to your father's sermons. There you sing, and learn that love is the most important thing in the world, and that you should treat everyone—black and white—as if they were your brothers and sisters.

These are all wonderful lessons that help you feel better about what happened to you at the shoe store.

The End

Many blacks in the city are very upset about **41** the arrest. Tired of the way they are being treated, someone suggests a *boycott*—refusing to ride on the buses at all.

In the evening there is a big meeting about what to do. Some members suggest approaching the city leaders. "We must not take drastic action," they say. Others wish to boycott the buses. The discussion goes back and forth.

One thing everyone agrees on is that *you* should be the leader and make the decision.

If you agree to lead the bus boycott, turn to page 24.

If you decide to call a meeting with the city leaders, turn to page 15.

The moon casts a pale band of light across your blanket, and you begin to dream that you are Martin Luther King, Jr. You are six years old. You run across the street to play with your two best friends. They are white. You knock on the door and ask their mother if they can come out and play.

"I'm sorry, but you can't play with my children anymore," she says and shuts the door.

You run home to your parents as fast as you can. You are upset by what happened. "Why can't I play with my friends anymore?" you ask. "We always play together."

Turn to page 18.

44   As much as you like playing with your cousins, you are anxious to try the rides. The next morning you are very excited. You talk of nothing else at the breakfast table as you try to decide which ride you want to go on first.

When you arrive at the amusement park, you run right up to the entrance booth. "Two tickets, please," you say eagerly.

The man in the booth gives you a very strange look. "Sorry," he says, pointing. "Don't you see the sign? It says, Whites Only."

"But why? I want to ride on the roller coaster and play in the fun house."

"I'm surprised *you* don't know the rules," the man says to your father.

Turn to page 26.

46   You decide to spend the day with your cousins. The next morning, bright and early, you are woken up by your mother as she lays out your clothes for the day.

After breakfast you and your family wait for the bus. It pulls up to the curb rather suddenly. Dust blows from the road onto your clothes.

The front of the bus is empty, but the back of the bus is full. All of the people sitting in the back are black. You and your family decide to sit down in the front.

At the next stop a white family stands, waiting for the bus. Before they even enter, the bus driver yells to your father, "You'll have to give up those seats now. You're going to have to stand."

If you do as you are told and stand, turn to page 53.

If you refuse to stand, turn to page 54.

Equal rights in Birmingham is only the first step in your fight for equality in America. The president of the United States calls for a law that would end segregation in all public places, but he needs support. You organize a great march to Washington, D.C., where tens of thousands of people come out to listen to you. In your speech you share your dream of a better world where all children will one day be judged not by the color of their skin, but for who they are. You say:

"I have a dream that one day . . . little black boys and black girls will be able to join hands with little white boys and white girls as sisters and brothers. I have a dream today!"

These words come straight from your heart into the hearts of all those who listen. Your hope is that they too can share in your dream.

Turn to page 32.

50   One night you get a call from someone threatening your life. You decide, for the safety of your family, that you should step down as leader.

Your family is asleep, and you are feeling all alone. You decide that you have to call on God for help. So you pray, asking for help in your struggle.

"I must confess that I'm weak right now. And I can't let the people see me like this because if they see me weak and losing my courage, then they too will begin to get weak."

As you pray, you feel yourself gaining more confidence. You feel that God will always be with you, helping you and your people in your fight for what is right. At once your fears leave you and you regain the courage to continue.

You will always remember this night when you are feeling sad and alone.

The End

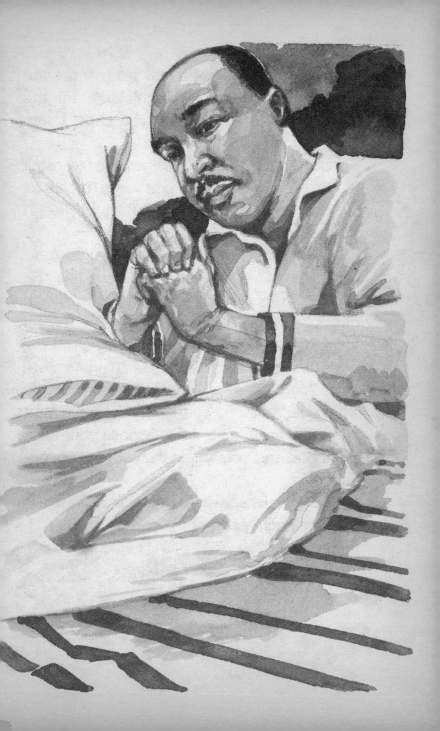

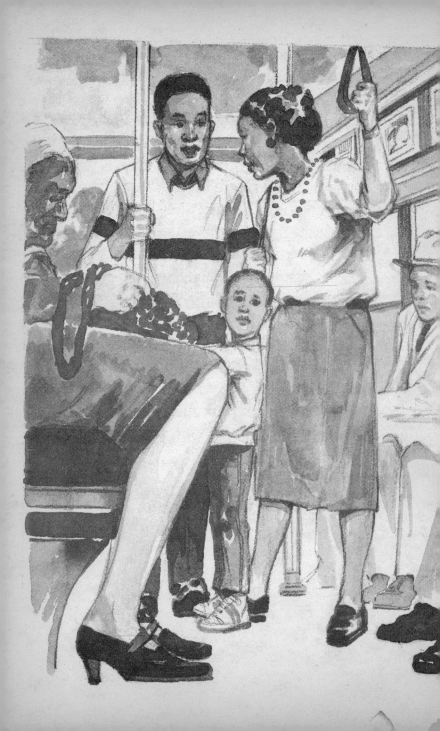

You and your family do as the bus driver **53** says and stand.

"Why is this happening?" you ask. "Why do we have to give up our seats just because we're black?"

"Ever since blacks were brought here from Africa and sold into slavery, they have been treated unfairly," your mother says sadly.

"But that was hundreds of years ago, wasn't it? There are no slaves anymore."

"I know, dear, but things are still very unfair. It's going to take someone very special to make all the changes that are needed— someone who can help the world to understand that all people are equal."

As you stand looking out the window, you wonder what, if anything, *you* could do to make a difference.

The End

54   You refuse to stand. "But these are *our* seats," you say indignantly.

"You heard the bus driver," your father says.

"What's the problem here? I told you to get up," the bus driver says once again.

By this time the white family enters the bus one by one. They stop in front of you. You remain seated, your arms folded across your chest. You are determined to keep your seat. The white man then demands that you get up, and the bus driver stands over you, frowning. With one tug he pulls you out of the seat and pushes you toward the back.

You are *very* angry. "One day things will change," you say. "You'll see, one day . . ."

It is then that you wake up with a start. You realize it was all a dream. The next morning, as you get on the bus to go to school, you take pride in knowing that, because of Martin Luther King, Jr., you can sit wherever you want.

The End

ABOUT THE AUTHOR

Anne Bailey was born in Jamaica, West Indies, and has lived in New York City for the past fourteen years, where she continues to pursue her writing and educational efforts. She has a strong interest in public education and has worked at the New York City Board of Education in several capacities. Ms. Bailey has contributed to *Return to the Cave of Time* in the Choose Your Own Adventure series. This is her first book.

ABOUT THE ILLUSTRATOR

Leslie Morrill is a designer and illustrator whose work has won him numerous awards. He has illustrated over thirty books for children, including the Bantam Classic edition of *The Wind in the Willows*. Mr. Morrill has illustrated many books in the Skylark Choose Your Own Adventure series, including *Home in Time for Christmas, You See the Future,* and *Stranded!* He has also illustrated *Mountain Survival, Invaders of the Planet Earth, The Brilliant Dr. Wogan, Mystery of the Sacred Stones, The Perfect Planet, The First Olympics, Hurricane!, Inca Gold,* and *Stock Car Champion* in the Choose Your Own Adventure series. Mr. Morrill also illustrated both Super Adventure books, *Journey to the Year 3000* and *Danger Zones.*

CHOOSE YOUR OWN ADVENTURE®

SKYLARK EDITIONS

- - - - - - - - - - - - - - - - - -

Bantam Books, Dept. AVSK, 414 East Golf Road, Des Plaines, IL 60016

Please send me the items I have checked above. I am enclosing $_____
(please add $2.00 to cover postage and handling). Send check or money
order, no cash or C.O.D.s please.

Mr/Ms _____

Address _____

City/State _____ Zip _____

AVSK-2/90

Please allow four to six weeks for delivery.
Prices and availability subject to change without notice.